Make a
MOUNTAIN
RANGE

By William Anthony

Minneapolis, Minnesota

Credits

Cover – Vixit, Alfie Photography, MaryDesy, Rhoeo, PictuLandra, Andreas Nesslinger, ectortatu. 4–5 – Vixit, Mike Pellinni. 6–7 – Punnawit Suwattananun, Sean Xu. 8–9 – MaryDesy, GN.Studio, Anett Gal, KittyVector. 10–11 – Rasto SK, Vixit. 12–13 – r.classen, Daniel Prudek. 14–15 – Multigon, Deni_Sugandi, Oleg_kelt. 16–17 – Janos Levente, Dzmitrock, Rob Crandall. 18–19 – Coulter J. Schmit, AB Photographie, Dennis W Donohue, Steve Boice, Rhoeo, Nadzin. 20–21 – Inspiring, Meiqianbao, Gorgev, Jamling Tenzing Norgay, CC BY-SA 3.0 <https://creativecommons.org/licenses/by-sa/3.0>, via Wikimedia Commons. 22–23 – Yana_z, frozenbunn.

Library of Congress Cataloging-in-Publication Data is available at www.loc.gov or upon request from the publisher.

ISBN: 978-1-63691-921-8 (hardcover)
ISBN: 978-1-63691-927-0 (paperback)
ISBN: 978-1-63691-933-1 (ebook)

© 2023 Booklife Publishing
This edition is published by arrangement with Booklife Publishing.

North American adaptations © 2023 Bearport Publishing Company. All rights reserved. No part of this publication may be reproduced in whole or in part, stored in any retrieval system, or transmitted in any form or by any means, electronic, mechanical, photocopying, recording, or otherwise, without written permission from the publisher.

For more information, write to Bearport Publishing, 5357 Penn Avenue South, Minneapolis, MN 55419. Printed in the United States of America.

Contents

How to Build Our World 4
Start at the Base 6
Set Up the Snow Line 8
Put On the Peak 10
Expand the Range 12
Heat Things Up 14
Place the Plants 16
Add the Animals 18
Create a Camp 20
Make Your Own Environment . . . 22
Glossary 24
Index 24

How to Build Our World

Our world is amazing. It is full of places to go and things to see. There are different **environments**, from mountains to deserts. Each one has plants, animals, and more.

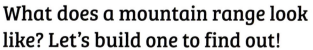
What does a mountain range look like? Let's build one to find out!

Start at the Base

A mountain range is a line of many mountains. But let's start with just one mountain. We'll build it from the ground up!

The bottom of a mountain is called the base.

The base of a mountain is warm enough for animals and plants to live there.

The land around the base often has small hills.

Set Up the Snow Line

Let's keep building upward. Next, we'll make the middle part of our mountain.

Snow line

The middle part of a mountain has snow only sometimes. This is because it is below the snow line. Places above the snow line have snow all year.

As we go farther up the mountain, the **temperature** gets colder and colder.

The middle part of a mountain is **steeper** than the base.

Put On the Peak

We'll finish building our mountain with a pointy peak. The top of a mountain always has a peak.

> The peak is the coldest part of a mountain. It is above the snow line, so it always has snow.

Because the peak is so high up, the air around it can be hard for people to breathe.

On many mountains, the peak is very steep and dangerous.

Expand the Range

Our first mountain looks great! Now, it's time to make the rest of the mountain range.

There are mountain ranges on every **continent**. The Himalayas are in Asia. The Rocky Mountains are in North America.

The longest mountain range that stretches across land is the Andes in South America.

Every mountain in a range is different. Some are steeper or taller than others.

Heat Things Up

Most mountains are made of **solid** rock. But not all mountains are like this. Let's add a volcano to our mountain range!

A volcano is a mountain that has a hole in the top or side. The hole goes deep below Earth's **surface.**

Sometimes, volcanoes erupt. This means lava comes out of the hole.

Lava is hot, **melted** rock. When it cools down, it becomes solid rock.

Place the Plants

Next, we'll put some plants on our mountain range. Each part of a mountain has different plants.

Trees, grasses, and flowers can all grow around the base of a mountain.

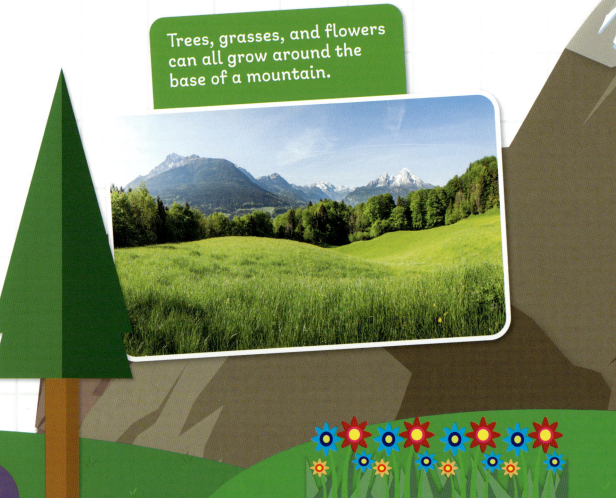

Add the Animals

The plants on our mountain range will make a great home for the next thing we need to add—animals!

Lots of different animals can live at the base of a mountain. There may be grizzly bears or red pandas.

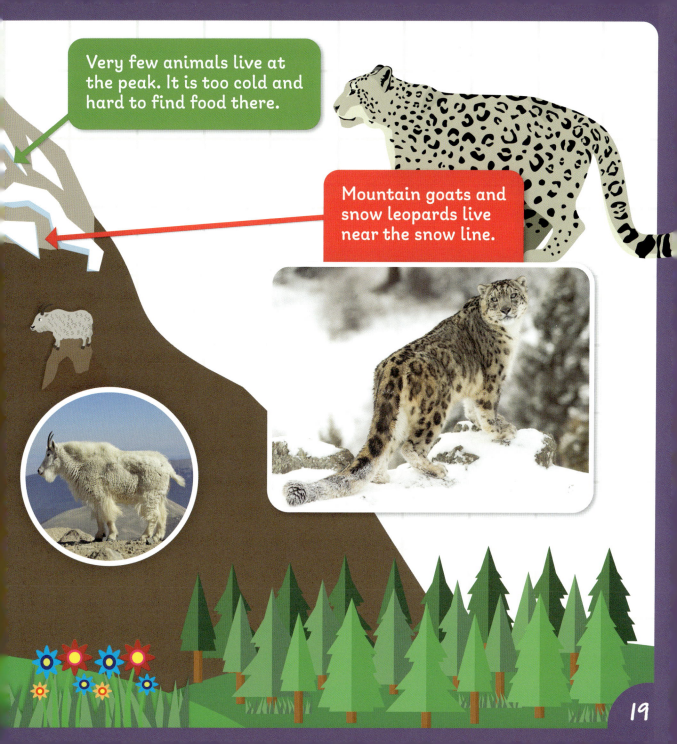

Create a Camp

Our mountains look so awesome that people will want to climb them. Let's set up a camp at the base.

People stay at a base camp when they are getting ready to climb a mountain.

People use special tools and **equipment** to stay safe.

Mount Everest is the world's tallest mountain. The first people climbed to its peak in 1953.

21

Make Your Own Environment

Mountain ranges are incredible! They have awesome animals, terrific trees, and cool camps. Now, it's time to build your own environment! You could draw it, paint it, or write about it. What do you want to put in your mountain range?

How many mountains will be in your range?

Will you add a giant volcano?

What will your base camp be like?

Glossary

continent one of the world's seven large land masses

environments the different parts of our world in which people, animals, and plants live

equipment helpful things that are used for a certain activity or job

melted turned to liquid because of heat

solid hard or firm

steeper rising more sharply

surface the top part of something

survive to stay alive

temperature how hot or cold something is

Index

air 11
animals 4, 6, 18–19, 22
base 6–7, 9, 16, 18, 20, 23
camps 20, 22–23
heat 14–15
peak 10–11, 17, 19, 21
snow 8, 10, 19
trees 16–17, 22
volcanoes 14–15, 23